WE
MORE NUTS!

To Jennifer. I'm nuts for you—JF

PENGUIN WORKSHOP
An Imprint of Penguin Random House LLC, New York

 Previously published in 2017 by Penguin Young Readers. This paperback edition published in 2019 by Penguin Workshop, an imprint of Penguin Random House LLC, New York. PENGUIN and PENGUIN WORKSHOP are trademarks of Penguin Books Ltd, and the W colophon is a registered trademark of Penguin Random House LLC. Manufactured in China.

Visit us online at www.penguinrandomhouse.com.

Library of Congress Control Number: 2017029202

ISBN 9780593095997 10 9 8 7 6 5 4 3 2 1

by Jonathan Fenske

Penguin Workshop

One nut.
Two nuts.
Three nuts.
Four nuts.

3
4

We have four nuts.

WE NEED MORE NUTS!

Five
and six
and seven
and eight.
Fun. Fun. Fun!
These nuts are
GREAT!

Eight nuts.
Great nuts!
Four...

...plus four.

Eight is great, but let's get MORE!

WHOA!

Nine nuts!
Ten nuts!
Twelve nuts!
DOINK!

10
12

Where did nut
ELEVEN go?

We’ve lost the nut that follows ten.

So spit them out. We'll start again!
12

One,
two,
three,
four,
five,
six,
seven.

Eight, nine, ten.

3
2
4
1
5

Should I go on?

Yes, yes! Please do!

Our old friend twelve.
Where one...
12

13

...meets two!
12

Thirteen.
Fourteen.
Fifteen.
Yay!
14
15

We're going nuts for nuts today!

Here. Sixteen nuts to fill your cheeks.
16

These nuts should keep us fed for weeks!
CALENDAR

Seventeen.
Eighteen.
Nineteen.
Twenty.
20
19
18
17

Should we get more?

SCHMARRGAWUMPHWOONAH!*

***NO! WE HAVE PLENTY!**

Aw, you're no fun.
Here's twenty-one.

And twenty-two.

And twenty-three.

I love these nuts!
I love this tree!

You're doing GREAT, my furry brother!

Open wide.

Twenty-four nuts!
YIPPEE-DEE!

THWACK!

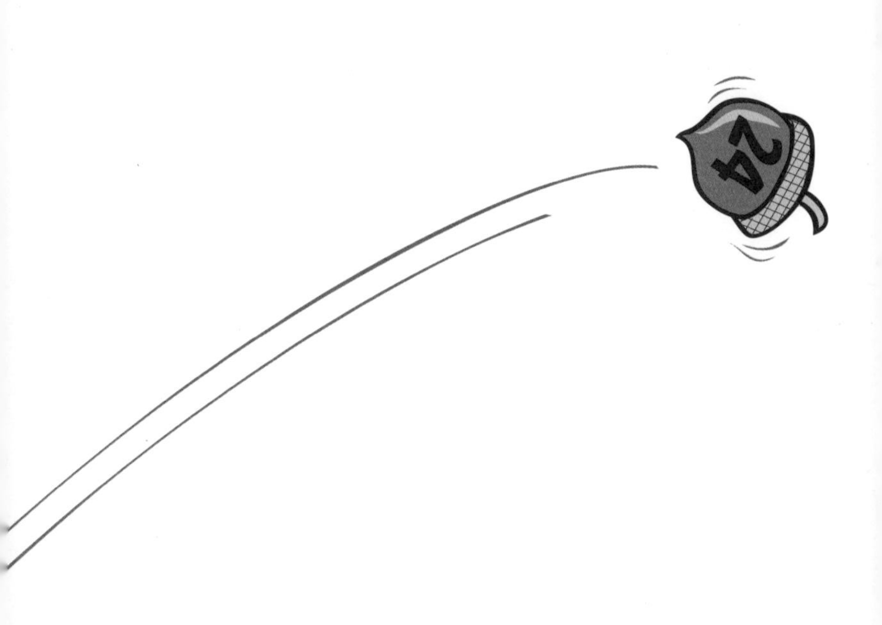
24

I guess we'll stop at TWENTY-THREE.